Robert Louis Stevenson

**Fables**

Robert Louis Stevenson

**Fables**

ISBN/EAN: 9783337075736

Printed in Europe, USA, Canada, Australia, Japan

Cover: Foto ©Andreas Hilbeck / pixelio.de

More available books at **www.hansebooks.com**

# FABLES.

# FABLES

BY

ROBERT LOUIS STEVENSON

NEW YORK

CHARLES SCRIBNER'S SONS

MDCCCXCVI

# INTRODUCTORY NOTE

THE fable, as a form of literary art, had at all times a great attraction for Mr. Stevenson; and in an early review of Lord **Lytton's** *Fables in Song* he attempted **to define** some **of** its proper **aims and** methods. **To** this class of work, according **to his** conception **of** the matter, belonged essentially **several of his** own semi-supernatural stories, such as "Will of the Mill," "Markheim," and **even** "Jekyll **and** Hyde;" **in the** composition of which there was combined **with** the dream element, **in at least an** equal **measure, the** element **of** moral allegory **or** apologue. He was accustomed also to try his hand occasionally **on the composition** of fables more strictly so called, and **cast in** the conventional brief and familiar form. By **the winter of** 1887–88 **he** had enough of these by him, together **with a** few others running to greater length, and conceived in a more **mystic** and legendary **vein, to** enable him, as he thought, to see **his way** towards making a **book** of them. Such **a** book he promised to Messrs. Longman **on** the occasion of a **visit** paid him in New York by a member of the firm in the spring of 1888. Then came his voyage to the Pacific and residence at Samoa. Among the multitude of new interests and images which filled his mind during the last six years of his life, he seems to have given little thought to the proposed book of fables. One or two, however, as will be seen, were added to the collection during this period. That collection, as it stood at the time of his death, was certainly not what its author had meant it to be. Whether it would have seen the light had he lived is doubtful; but after his death it seemed to his representatives of sufficient interest to be handed to Messrs. Longman, in part fulfilment of his old pledge to them, for publication in their Magazine, and there it first appeared.

S. C.

# CONTENTS

| | PAGE |
|---|---|
| I. THE PERSONS OF THE TALE, | 3 |
| II. THE SINKING SHIP, | 10 |
| III. THE TWO MATCHES, | 14 |
| IV. THE SICK MAN AND THE FIREMAN, | 16 |
| V. THE DEVIL AND THE INNKEEPER, | 18 |
| VI. THE PENITENT, | 20 |
| VII. THE YELLOW PAINT, | 21 |
| VIII. THE HOUSE OF ELD, | 26 |
| IX. THE FOUR REFORMERS, | 38 |
| X. THE MAN AND HIS FRIEND, | 40 |
| XI. THE READER, | 42 |
| XII. THE CITIZEN AND THE TRAVELLER, | 44 |
| XIII. THE DISTINGUISHED STRANGER, | 45 |
| XIV. THE CARTHORSES AND THE SADDLEHORSE, | 48 |
| XV. THE TADPOLE AND THE FROG, | 50 |

PAGE

XVI. SOMETHING IN IT, .    .    .    . 51

XVII. FAITH, HALF - FAITH, AND NO

FAITH AT ALL,    .    .    . 57

XVIII. THE TOUCHSTONE,    .    .    . 61

XIX. THE POOR THING, .    .    .    . 74

XX. THE SONG OF THE MORROW,    . 85

# FABLES

# FABLES.

---

## *THE PERSONS OF THE TALE.*

AFTER the 32nd chapter of *Treasure Island*, two of the puppets strolled out to have a pipe before business should begin again, and met in an open place not far from the story.

"Good morning, Cap'n," said the first, with a man-o'-war salute and a beaming countenance.

"Ah, Silver!" grunted the other. "You're in a bad way, Silver."

"Now, Cap'n Smollett," remonstrated Silver, "dooty is dooty, as I knows, and none better; but we're off dooty now; and I can't see no call to keep up the morality business."

"You're a damned rogue, my man," said the Captain.

"Come, come, Cap'n, be just," returned the other. "There's no call to be angry with me in earnest. I'm on'y a chara'ter in a sea story. I don't really exist."

"Well, I don't really exist either," says the Captain, "which seems to meet that."

"I wouldn't set no limits to what a virtuous chara'ter might consider argument," responded Silver. "But I'm the villain of this tale, I am; and speaking as one seafaring man to another, what I want to know is, what's the odds?"

"Were you never taught your catechism?" said the Captain. "Don't you know there's such a thing as an Author?"

"Such a thing as a Author?" returned John, derisively. "And who better'n me? And the p'int is, if the Author made you, he made Long John, and he made Hands, and Pew, and George Merry—not that George is up to much, for he's little more'n a name; and he made Flint, what there is of him; and he made this here mutiny, you keep such a work

about; and he had Tom Redruth shot; and—
well, if that's a Author, give me Pew!"

"Don't you believe in a future state?"
said Smollett. "Do you think there's nothing
but the present story-paper?"

"I don't rightly know for that," said Silver; "and I don't see what it's got to do
with it, anyway. What I know is this: if there
is sich a thing as a Author, I'm his favourite
chara'ter. He does me fathoms better'n he
does you—fathoms, he does. And he likes
doing me. He keeps me on deck mostly all
the time, crutch and all; and he leaves you
measling in the hold, where nobody can't see
you, nor wants to, and you may lay to that!
If there is a Author, by thunder, but he's on
my side, and you may lay to it!"

"I see he's giving you a long rope," said
the Captain. "But that can't change a man's
convictions. I know the author respects me;
I feel it in my bones; when you and I had
that talk at the blockhouse door, who do you
think he was for, my man?"

"And don't he respect me?" cried Silver.
"Ah, you should 'a' heard me putting down

my mutiny, George Merry and Morgan and
that lot, no longer ago'n last chapter ; you'd 'a'
heard something then ! You'd 'a' seen what the
Author thinks o' me ! But come now, do you
consider yourself a virtuous chara'ter clean
through ? "

" God forbid ! " said Captain Smollett sol-
emnly. " I am a man that tries to do his
duty, and makes a mess of it as often as not.
I'm not a very popular man at home, Silver,
I'm afraid," and the Captain sighed.

" Ah," says Silver. " Then how about this
sequel of yours? Are you to be Cap'n Smollett just the same as ever, and not very popular
at home, says you ! And if so, why it's *Treasure Island* over again, by thunder ; and I'll be
Long John, and Pew'll be Pew ; and we'll
have another mutiny, as like as not. Or are
you to be somebody else? And if so, why,
what the better are you? and what the worse
am I ? "

" Why, look here, my man," returned the
Captain, " I can't understand how this story
comes about at all, can I? I can't see how
you and I, who don't exist, should get to speak-

ing here, and smoke our pipes, for all the world like reality? Very well, then, who am I to pipe up with my opinions? I know the Author's on the side of good; he tells me so, it runs out of his pen as he writes. Well, that's all I need to know; I'll take my chance upon the rest."

"It's a fact he seemed to be against George Merry," Silver admitted musingly. "But George is little more'n a name at the best of it," he added brightening. "And to get into soundings for once. What is this good? I made a mutiny, and I been a gentleman o' fortune; well, but by all stories, you ain't no such saint. I'm a man that keeps company very easy; even by your own account, you ain't, and to my certain knowledge, you're a devil to haze. Which is which? Which is good, and which bad? Ah, you tell me that! Here we are in stays, and you may lay to it!"

"We're none of us perfect," replied the Captain. "That's a fact of religion, my man. All I can say is, I try to do my duty; and if you try to do yours, I can't compliment you on your success."

"And so you was the judge, was you?" said
Silver, derisively.

"I would be both judge and hangman for
you, my man, and never turn a hair," returned
the Captain. "But I get beyond that: it
mayn't be sound theology, but it's common
sense, that what is good is useful too—or there
and thereabout, for I don't set up to be a
thinker. Now, where would a story go to, if
there were no virtuous characters?"

"If you go to that," replied Silver, "where
would a story begin, if there wasn't no vil-
lains?"

"Well, that's pretty much my thought,"
said Captain Smollett. "The author has to
get a story; that's what he wants; and to get
a story, and to have a man like the doctor (say)
given a proper chance, he has to put in men
like you and Hands. But he's on the right
side; and you mind your eye! You're not
through this story yet; there's trouble coming
for you."

"What'll you bet?" asked John.

"Much I care if there ain't," returned the
Captain. "I'm glad enough to be Alexander

Smollett, bad as he is ; **and I thank** my stars upon my knees that I'm not Silver.    But there's the ink-bottle opening.    To quarters ! ''

And indeed the author was **just then** begining to write the words :

## CHAPTER XXXIII.

## THE SINKING SHIP.

"SIR," said the first lieutenant, bursting into the Captain's cabin, "the ship is going down."

"Very well, Mr. Spoker," said the Captain; "but that is no reason for going about half-shaved. Exercise your mind a moment, Mr. Spoker, and you will see that to the philosophic eye there is nothing new in our position: the ship (if she is to go down at all) may be said to have been going down siuce she was launched."

"She is settling fast," said the first lieutenant, as he returned from shaving.

"Fast, Mr. Spoker?" asked the Captain. "The expression is a strange one, for time (if you will think of it) is only relative."

"Sir," said the lieutenant, "I think it is scarcely worth while to embark in such a discussion when we shall all **be in** Davy Jones's Locker in **ten** minutes.''

"By parity of reasoning," returned the Captain gently, "it would never be worth while to begin any inquiry of importance; the odds are always overwhelming that we must die before we shall have brought it to an end. You have not considered, Mr. Spoker, the situation of man," said the Captain, smiling and shaking his head.

"I am much more engaged **in** considering the position of the ship," said **Mr.** Spoker.

"Spoken like **a** good officer," replied the Captain, laying his hand on the lieutenant's shoulder.

On deck they found the men had broken into the spirit-room, and **were** fast getting drunk.

"My men," said the Captain, "there is **no** sense in this. The **ship is** going down, you will tell me, in ten minutes: well, and what then? To the philosophic eye, there is nothing new in our position. All our lives long, we may have been about to break a bloodvessel or to be struck by lightning, not merely in ten

minutes, but in ten seconds; and that has not
prevented us from eating dinner, no, nor from
putting money in the Savings Bank. I assure
you, with my hand on my heart, I fail to com-
prehend your attitude."

The men were already too far gone to pay
much heed.

" This is a very painful sight, Mr. Spoker,"
said the Captain.

" And yet to the philosophic eye, or what-
ever it is," replied the first lieutenant, " they
may be said to have been getting drunk since
they came aboard."

" I do not know if you always follow my
thought, Mr. Spoker," returned the Captain
gently.  " But let us proceed."

In the powder magazine they found an old
salt smoking his pipe.

" Good God," cried the Captain, " what are
you about?"

" Well, sir," said the old salt, apologetically,
" they told me as she were going down."

" And suppose she were?" said the Captain.
" To the philosophic eye, there would be
nothing new in our position. Life, my old

shipmate, life, at any moment and in any view, is as dangerous as a sinking ship; and yet it is man's handsome fashion to carry umbrellas, to wear indiarubber overshoes, **to** begin vast works, and **to** conduct himself **in** every way **as** if he might hope to be eternal. And for **my** own poor part **I** should despise the man who, even on board a sinking ship, should omit to take a pill or to wind **up** his watch. That, my friend, would not be the human attitude."

"I beg pardon, sir," said **Mr.** Spoker. "But what is precisely the difference between shaving in a sinking ship **and** smoking in a powder magazine?"

"Or doing anything **at** all in any conceivable circumstances?" cried **the** Captain. "Perfectly conclusive; give me **a** cigar!"

Two minutes afterwards the ship **blew up** with a glorious detonation.

## THE TWO MATCHES.

ONE day there was a traveller in the woods in California, in the dry season, when the Trades were blowing strong. He had ridden a long way, and he was tired and hungry, and dismounted from his horse to smoke a pipe. But when he felt in his pocket, he found but two matches. He struck the first, and it would not light.

"Here is a pretty state of things," said the traveller. "Dying for a smoke; only one match left; and that certain to miss fire! Was there ever a creature so unfortunate? And yet," thought the traveller, "suppose I light this match, and smoke my pipe, and shake out the dottle here in the grass—the grass might catch on fire, for it is dry like tinder; and while I snatch out the flames in front, they might evade and run behind me, and seize upon yon bush of poison oak ; before I could reach it, that would have blazed up ; over the bush I see a pine tree hung with moss ; that too would fly in fire upon the instant to its topmost bough ; and the flame of that long torch—how would the trade wind take and brandish that through the inflammable forest ! I hear this dell roar in a moment with the joint voice of wind and fire, I see myself gallop for my soul, and the flying conflagration chase and outflank me through the hills ; I see this pleasant forest burn for days, and the cattle roasted, and the springs dried up, and the farmer ruined, and his children cast upon the world. What a world hangs upon this moment ! "

With that he struck the match, and it missed fire.

" Thank God," said the traveller, and put his pipe in his pocket.

## THE SICK MAN AND THE FIRE-MAN.

THERE was once a sick man in a burning house, to whom there entered a fireman.

"Do not save me," said the sick man. "Save those who are strong."

"Will you kindly tell me why?" inquired the fireman, for he was a civil fellow.

"Nothing could possibly be fairer," said the sick man. "The strong should be preferred in all cases, because they are of more service in the world."

The fireman pondered a while, for he was a man of some philosophy. "Granted," said he at last, as a part of the roof fell in; "but for the sake of conversation, what would you lay down as the proper service of the strong?"

"Nothing can possibly be easier," returned

the sick man : " the proper service of the strong is to help the weak."

Again the fireman reflected, **for** there was nothing hasty about this excellent creature. " I could forgive you being sick," he said **at** last, as a portion of the wall **fell** out, " **but I** cannot bear your being such a fool." And with **that he** heaved up **his** fireman's axe, **for he was** eminently just, **and clove** the sick **man to the** bed.

2

## *THE DEVIL AND THE INN-KEEPER.*

ONCE upon a time the devil stayed at an inn, where no one knew him, for they were people whose education had been neglected. He was bent on mischief, and for a time kept everybody by the ears. But at last the innkeeper set a watch upon the devil and took him in the fact.

The inkeeper got a rope's end.

" Now I am going to thrash you," said the innkeeper.

" You have no right to be angry with me," said the devil. " I am only the devil, and it is my nature to do wrong."

" Is that so ? " asked the innkeeper.

" Fact, I assure you," said the devil.

" You really cannot help doing ill ? " asked the innkeeper.

" Not in the smallest," said the devil ; " it would be useless cruelty to thrash a thing like me."

" It would indeed," said the innkeeper.

And he made a noose and hanged the devil.

" There," said the innkeeper.

## THE PENITENT.

A MAN met a lad weeping. "What do you weep for?" he asked.

"I am weeping for my sins," said the lad.

"You must have little to do," said the man.

The next day they met again. Once more the lad was weeping. "Why do you weep now?" asked the man.

"I am weeping because I have nothing to eat," said the lad.

"I thought it would come to that," said the man.

## *THE YELLOW PAINT.*

IN a certain city, there lived a physician who sold yellow paint. This was of so singular a virtue that whoso was bedaubed with it from head to heel was set free from the dangers of life, and the bondage of sin, and the fear of death forever. So the physician said in his prospectus ; and so said all the citizens in the city ; and there was nothing more urgent in men's hearts than to be properly painted themselves, and nothing they took more delight in than to see others painted. There was in the same city a young man of a very good family but of a somewhat reckless life ; who had reached the age of manhood and would have nothing to say to the paint : " To-morrow was soon enough," said he ; and when the morrow came he would still put it off. So he might have continued to do until his death ; only, he had a friend of

about his own age and much of his own manners ; and this youth, taking a walk in the pub-
lic street, with not one fleck of paint upon his
body, was suddenly run down by a watercart
and cut off in the heyday of his nakedness.
This shook the other to the soul; so that I
never beheld a man more earnest to be painted ;
and on the very same evening, in the presence
of all his family, to appropriate music, and himself weeping aloud, he received three complete
coats and a touch of varnish on the top.   The
physician (who was himself affected even to
tears) protested he had never done a job so
thorough.

Some two months afterwards, the young man
was carried on a stretcher to the physician's
house.

" What is the meaning of this ? " he cried, as
soon as the door was opened.   "I was to be
set free from all the dangers of life ; and here
have I been run down by that self-same watercart, and my leg is broken."

" Dear me ! " said the physician.   " This
is very sad.   But I perceive I must explain to
you the action of my paint.   A broken bone

is a mighty small affair at the worst of it ; and
it belongs to a class **of** accidents to which my
paint is quite inapplicable. Sin, my dear
young friend, sin is the sole calamity that a wise
man should apprehend ; it is against sin that I
have fitted you out ; and when you come to be
tempted, you will give me news of my paint ! "

" O ! " said the young man, " I did not
understand that, and it seems rather disappointing. But I have no doubt all is for the best ;
and in the meanwhile, I shall be obliged to you
if you will set my leg."

" That is none of my business," said the
physician ; " but if your bearers will carry you
round the corner to the surgeon's, I feel sure he
will afford relief."

Some three years later, the young man came
running to the physician's house in a great per-
turbation. " What is the meaning of this ? "
he cried. " Here was I to be set free from the
bondage of sin ; and I have just committed
forgery, arson and murder."

" Dear me," said the physician. " This is
very serious. Off with your clothes at once."
And as soon as the young man had stripped, he

examined him from head to foot. "No," he cried with great relief, "there is not a flake broken. Cheer up, my young friend, your paint is as good as new."

"Good God!" cried the young man, "and what then can be the use of it?"

"Why," said the physician, "I perceive I must explain to you the nature of the action of my paint. It does not exactly prevent sin; it extenuates instead the painful consequences. It is not so much for this world as for the next; it is not against life; in short, it is against death that I have fitted you out. And when you come to die, you will give me news of my paint."

"O!" cried the young man, "I had not understood that, and it seems a little disappointing. But, there, no doubt all is for the best: and in the meanwhile, I shall be obliged if you will help me to undo the evil I have brought on innocent persons."

"That is none of my business," said the physician; "but if you will go round the corner to the police office, I feel sure it will afford you relief to give yourself up."

Six weeks later, the physician was called to the town gaol.

" What is the meaning of this? " cried the young man. " Here am I literally crusted with your paint; and I have broken my leg, and committed all the crimes in the calendar, and must be hanged to-morrow ; and am in the meanwhile in a fear so extreme that I lack words to picture it."

" Dear me," said the physician. " This is really amazing. Well, well ; perhaps, if you had not been painted, you would have been more frightened still."

## *THE HOUSE OF ELD.*

SO soon as the child began to speak, the gyve was riveted; and the boys and girls limped about their play like convicts. Doubtless it was more pitiable to see and more painful to bear in youth; but even the grown folk, besides being very unhandy on their feet, were often sick with ulcers.

About the time when Jack was ten years old, many strangers began to journey through that country. These he beheld going lightly by on the long roads, and the thing amazed him. "I wonder how it comes," he asked, "that all these strangers are so quick afoot, and we must drag about our fetter."

"My dear boy," said his uncle, the catechist, "do not complain about your fetter, for it is the only thing that makes life worth living. None are happy, none are good, none are respectable, that are not gyved like us. And I must tell you, besides, it is very dangerous talk. If you grumble of your iron, you will have no luck ; **if** ever you take it off, you will be instantly smitten by **a** thunderbolt."

"Are there no thunderbolts for these strangers?" asked Jack.

"Jupiter is longsuffering to the benighted," returned the catechist.

"Upon my word, I could wish I had **been** less fortunate," said Jack. "For if I had been born benighted, I might now be going free; and it cannot be denied the iron is inconvenient, and the ulcer hurts."

"Ah!" cried his uncle, "do not envy the heathen! Theirs is a sad lot! Ah, poor souls, if they but knew the joys **of** being fettered! Poor souls, my heart yearns for them. But **the** truth is they are vile, odious, insolent, ill-conditioned, stinking brutes, not truly human—for what is a man without **a** fetter?—and you cannot be too particular not to touch or speak with them."

After this talk, the child would never pass one of the unfettered on the road but what he spat at him and called him names, which was the practice of the children in that part.

It chanced one day, when he was fifteen, he went into the woods, and the ulcer pained him. It was a fair day, with a blue sky; all the birds were singing; but Jack nursed his foot. Presently, another song began; it sounded like the singing of a person, only far more gay; at the same time, there was a beating on the earth. Jack put aside the leaves; and there was a lad of his own village, leaping, and dancing and singing to himself in a green dell; and on the grass beside him lay the dancer's iron.

"O!" cried Jack, "you have your fetter off!"

"For God's sake, don't tell your uncle!" cried the lad.

"If you fear my uncle," returned Jack, "why do you not fear the thunderbolt?"

"That is only an old wives' tale," said the other. "It is only told to children. Scores of us come here among the woods and dance for nights together, and are none the worse."

This put Jack in a thousand new thoughts. He was a grave lad; he had no mind to dance

himself; he wore his fetter manfully and tended
his ulcer without complaint.   But he loved the
less to be deceived or to see others cheated.  He
began to lie in wait for heathen travellers, at
covert parts of the road, and in the dusk of the
day, so that he might speak with them unseen ;
and these were greatly taken with their wayside
questioner, and told him things of weight.  The
wearing of gyves (they said) was no command
of Jupiter's.   It was the contrivance of a white-
faced thing, a sorcerer, that dwelt in that
country in the Wood of Eld.  He was one like
Glaucus that could change his shape, yet he
could be always told ;  for when he was crossed,
he gobbled like a turkey.   He had three lives ;
but the third smiting would make an end of
him indeed ;  and with that his house of sorcery
would vanish, the gyves fall, **and** the villagers
take hands and dance like children.

"And in your country ?" Jack would ask.

But at this the travellers, with one accord,
would put him off ; until Jack began to suppose
there was no land entirely happy.   Or, **if** there
were, it must be one that kept its folk at home ;
which was natural enough.

But the case of the gyves weighed upon him. The sight of the children limping stuck in his eyes ; the groans of such as dressed their ulcers haunted him. And it came at last in his mind that he was born to free them.

There was in that village a sword of heavenly forgery, beaten upon Vulcan's anvil. It was never used but in the temple, and then the flat of it only ; and it hung on a nail by the catechist's chimney. Early one night, Jack rose, and took the sword, and was gone out of the house and the village in the darkness.

All night he walked at a venture ; and when day came, he met strangers going to the fields. Then he asked after the Wood of Eld and the house of sorcery ; and one said north, and one south ; until Jack saw that they deceived him. So then, when he asked his way of any man, he showed the bright sword naked ; and at that the gyve on the man's ankle rang, and answered in his stead ; and the word was still *Straight on.* But the man, when his gyve spoke, spat and struck at Jack, and threw stones at him as he went away ; so that his head was broken.

So he came to that wood, and entered in,
and he was aware of a house in a low place,
where funguses grew, and the trees met, and
the steaming of the marsh arose about it like a
smoke. It was a fine house, and a very ram-
bling ; some parts of it were ancient like the
hills, and some but of yesterday, and none
finished ; and all the ends of it were open, so
that you could go in from every side. Yet
it was in good repair, and all the chimneys
smoked.

Jack went in through the gable ; and there
was one room after another, all bare, but all
furnished in part so that a man could dwell
there ; and in each there was a fire burning
where a man could warm himself, and a table
spread where he might eat. But Jack saw no-
where any living creature ; only the bodies of
some stuffed.

"This is a hospitable house," said Jack ;
"but the ground must be quaggy underneath,
for at every step the building quakes."

He had gone some time in the house, when
he began to be hungry. Then he looked at
the food, and at first he was afraid ; but he

bared the sword, and by the shining of the
sword, it seemed the food was honest. So he
took the courage to sit down and eat, and he
was refreshed in mind and body.

" This is strange," thought he, " that in the
house of sorcery, there should be food so wholesome."

As he was yet eating, there came into that
room the appearance of his uncle, and Jack was
afraid because he had taken the sword. But his
uncle was never more kind, and sat down to
meat with him, and praised him because he had
taken the sword. Never had these two been
more pleasantly together, and Jack was full of
love to the man.

" It was very well done," said his uncle,
" to take the sword and come yourself into the
House of Eld ; a good thought and a brave
deed. But now you are satisfied ; and we may
go home to dinner arm in arm."

" O, dear, no ! " said Jack. " I am not satisfied yet."

" How ! " cried his uncle. " Are you not
warmed by the fire ? Does not this food sus-
tain you ? "

" I see the food to be wholesome," said Jack, " and still it is no proof that a man should wear a gyve on his right leg."

Now at this the appearance **of** his uncle gobbled like a turkey.

" Jupiter ! " cried Jack, " is this the sorcerer ? "

His hand held back and his heart failed him for the love he bore his uncle ; but he heaved up the sword and smote the appearance on the head ; and it cried out aloud with the voice of his uncle ; and fell to the ground ; and a little bloodless white thing fled from the room.

The cry rang in Jack's ears, and his knees smote together, and conscience cried upon him ; and yet he was strengthened, and there woke in his bones the lust of that enchanter's blood. " If the gyves are to fall," said he, " I must go through with this, and when I get home, I shall find my uncle dancing."

So he went on after the bloodless thing. **In** the way, he **met the** appearance of his father ; and his father was incensed, and railed upon him, and called to him upon his duty, and bade him be home, while there was yet time.

"For you can still," said he, "be home by sunset; and then all will be forgiven."

"God knows," said Jack, "I fear your anger; but yet your anger does not prove that a man should wear a gyve on his right leg."

And at that the appearance of his father gobbled like a turkey.

"Ah, heaven," cried Jack, "the sorcerer again!"

The blood ran backward in his body and his joints rebelled against him for the love he bore his father; but he heaved up the sword, and plunged it in the heart of the appearance; and the appearance cried out aloud with the voice of his father; and fell to the ground; and a little bloodless white thing fled from the room.

The cry rang in Jack's ears, and his soul was darkened; but now rage came to him. "I have done what I dare not think upon," said he. "I will go to an end with it, or perish. And when I get home, I pray God this may be a dream and I may find my father dancing."

So he went on after the bloodless thing that had escaped; and in the way he met the appearance of his mother, and she wept. "What have **you** done?" she cried. "What is this **that you have done?** O, come home (where you may be by bedtime) ere you **do** more ill to me and mine; for it is enough to smite my brother and your father."

"Dear mother, it is not **these** that I have smitten," said Jack; "it was but the enchanter in their shape. And even if I had, it would not prove that a man should **wear a gyve on his** right leg."

**And at this** the appearance gobbled like a turkey.

He never knew how he did that; but he **swung** the sword on the one side, and clove the appearance through the midst; and it cried out aloud with the voice of his mother; and fell to the ground; and with the fall of it, the house was gone from over Jack's head, and **he** stood alone in the woods, and the gyve was loosened from his leg.

"Well," said he, "the enchanter is now dead **and** the fetter gone." But the cries rang in his soul, and the day was like night to him. "This **has** been **a sore** business," said **he.**

"Let me get forth out of the wood, and see the good that I have done to others."

He thought to leave the fetter where it lay, but when he turned to go, his mind was otherwise. So he stooped and put the gyve in his bosom ; and the rough iron galled him as he went, and his bosom bled.

Now when he was forth of the wood upon the highway, he met folk returning from the field ; and those he met had no fetter on the right leg, but behold ! they had one upon the left. Jack asked them what it signified ; and they said, " that was the new wear, for the old was found to be a superstition." Then he looked at them nearly ; and there was a new ulcer on the left ankle, and the old one on the right was not yet healed.

" Now may God forgive me ! " cried Jack, " I would I were well home."

And when he was home, there lay his uncle smitten on the head, and his father pierced through the heart, and his mother cloven through the midst. And he sat in the lone house and wept beside the bodies.

## *Moral.*

Old is the tree and the fruit good,
Very old and thick the wood.
Woodman, **is your courage stout?**
Beware ! the root is wrapped about
Your mother's heart, your father's bones ;
**And like the** mandrake comes with groans.

## IX

## THE FOUR REFORMERS.

FOUR reformers met under a bramble bush. They were all agreed the world must be changed. "We must abolish property," said one.

"We must abolish marriage," said the second.

"We must abolish God," said the third.

"I wish we could abolish work," said the fourth.

"Do not let us get beyond practical politics," said the first. "The first thing is to reduce men to a common level."

"The first thing," said the second, "is to give freedom to the sexes."

"The first thing," said the third, "is to find out how to do it."

"The first step," said the first, "is to abolish the Bible."

" The first thing," said the second, " is to abolish the laws."

" The first thing," said the third, " is to abolish mankind."

## X

## *THE MAN AND HIS FRIEND.*

A MAN quarrelled with his friend.
" I have been much deceived in you,"
said the man.

And the friend made a face at him and went
away.

A little after, they both died, and came together before the great white Justice of the
Peace. It began to look black for the friend,
but the man for a while had a clear character
and was getting in good spirits.

" I find here some record of a quarrel," said
the justice, looking in his notes. " Which of
you was in the wrong ? "

" He was," said the man. " He spoke ill
of me behind my back."

" Did he so ? " said the justice. " And pray
how did he speak about your neighbours ? "

"O, he had always a nasty tongue," said the man.

"And you chose him for your friend?" cried the justice. "My good fellow, we have no use here for fools."

So the man was cast in the pit, and the friend laughed out aloud in the dark and remained to be tried on other charges.

## XI

## THE READER.

" I NEVER read such an impious book,"
said the reader, throwing it on the
floor.

" You need not hurt me," said the book;
" you will only get less for me second hand,
and I did not write myself."

" That is true," said the reader. " My
quarrel is with your author."

" Ah, well," said the book, " you need not
buy his rant."

" That is true," said the reader. " But I
thought him such a cheerful writer."

" I find him so," said the book.

" You must be differently made from me,"
said the reader.

" Let me tell you a fable," said the book.
" There were two men wrecked upon a desert

island ; one of them made believe he was at home, the other admitted——"

"Oh, I know your kind of fable," said the reader. "They both died."

"And so they did," said the book. "No doubt of that. And everybody else."

"That is true," said the reader. "Push it a little further for this once. And when they were all dead ?"

"They were in God's hands the same as before," said the book.

"Not much to boast of, by your account," cried the reader.

"Who is impious now ?" said the book.

And the reader put him on the fire.

The coward crouches from the rod,
And loathes the iron face of God.

## XII.

### THE CITIZEN AND THE TRAVEL-LER.

" LOOK round you," said the citizen. "This is the largest market in the world."

" Oh, surely not," said the traveller.

"Well, perhaps not the largest," said the citizen, "but much the best."

"You are certainly wrong there," said the traveller. " I can tell you  .  .  ."

They buried the stranger at the dusk.

## XIII

## THE DISTINGUISHED STRANGER.

ONCE upon a time there came to this earth a visitor from a neighbouring planet. And he was met at the place of his descent by a great philosopher, who was to show him everything.

First of all they came through a wood, and the stranger looked upon the trees. "Whom have we here?" said he.

"These are only vegetables," said the philosopher. "They are alive, but not at all interesting."

"I don't know about that," said the stranger. "They seem to have very good manners. Do they never speak?"

"They lack the gift," said the philosopher.

"Yet I think I hear them sing," said the other.

"That is only the wind among the leaves,"

said the philosopher. "I will explain to you the theory of winds: it is very interesting."

"Well," said the stranger, "I wish I knew what they are thinking."

"They cannot think," said the philosopher.

"I don't know about that," returned the stranger: and then laying his hand upon a trunk: "I like these people," said he.

"They are not people at all," said the philosopher. "Come along."

Next they came through a meadow where there were cows.

"These are very dirty people," said the stranger.

"They are not people at all," said the philosopher; and he explained what a cow is in scientific words which I have forgotten.

"That is all one to me," said the stranger. "But why do they never look up?"

"Because they are graminivorous," said the philosopher; "and to live upon grass, which is not highly nutritious, requires so close an attention to business that they have no time to think, or speak, or look at the scenery, or keep themselves clean."

" Well," said the stranger, " that **is one way** to live, **no** doubt. **But I** prefer the people with the green heads."

**Next they** came **into** a city, **and** the streets were full of men and women.

" These are very odd **people,"** said **the** stranger.

" They are the people of the greatest nation in the world," said the philosopher.

" Are they indeed?" said **the stranger.** " They scarcely look **so."**

## XIV

## THE CARTHORSES AND THE SAD-
## DLEHORSE.

TWO carthorses, a gelding and a mare, were brought to Samoa, and put in the same field with a saddlehorse to run free on the island. They were rather afraid to go near him, for they saw he was a saddlehorse, and supposed he would not speak to them. Now the saddlehorse had never seen creatures so big. "These must be great chiefs," thought he, and he approached them civilly. "Lady and gentleman," said he, "I understand you are from the colonies. I offer you my affectionate compliments, and make you heartily welcome to the island."

The colonials looked at him askance, and consulted with each other.

"Who can he be?" said the gelding.

"He seems suspiciously civil," said the mare.

" I do not think he can be much account,"
said the gelding.

" Depend upon it he is only a Kanaka," said
the mare.

Then they turned to him.

" Go to the devil ! " said the gelding.

" I wonder at your impudence, speaking to
persons of our quality ! " cried the mare.

The saddlehorse went away by himself.  " I
was right," said he, " they are great chiefs."

4

## XV

## THE TADPOLE AND THE FROG.

"BE ashamed of yourself," said the frog. "When I was a tadpole, I had no tail."

"Just what I thought!" said the tadpole. "You never were a tadpole."

# XVI.

## *SOMETHING IN IT.*

THE natives told him many tales. In particular, they warned him of the house of yellow reeds tied with black sinnet, how anyone who touched it became instantly the prey of Akaänga, and was handed on to him by Miru the ruddy, and hocussed with the kava of the dead, and baked in the ovens and eaten by the eaters of the dead.

" There is nothing in it," said the missionary.

There was a bay upon that island, a very fair bay to look upon ; but, by the native saying, it was death to bathe there. " There is nothing in that," said the missionary ; and he came to the bay and went swimming. Presently an eddy took him and bore him towards the reef. " Oho ! " thought the missionary, " it seems there is something in it after all." And he swam the harder, but the eddy carried him away. "I do not care about this eddy," said the missionary; and even as he said it, he was aware of a house raised on piles above the sea; it was built of yellow reeds, one reed joined with another, and the whole bound with black sinnet; a ladder led to the door, and all about the house hung calabashes. He had never seen such a house, nor yet such calabashes; and the eddy set for the ladder. "This is singular," said the missionary, "but there can be nothing in it." And he laid hold of the ladder and went up. It was a fine house; but there was no man there; and when the missionary looked back he saw no island, only the heaving of the sea. "It is strange about the island," said the missionary, "but who's afraid? my stories are the true ones." And he laid hold of a calabash, for he was one that loved curiosities. Now he had no sooner laid hand upon the calabash than that which he handled, and that which he saw and stood on, burst like a bubble and was gone; and night closed upon him, and the waters, and the meshes of the net; and he wallowed there like a fish.

"A body would think there was something in this," said the missionary. "But if these tales are true, I wonder what about my tales!"

Now the flaming of Akaänga's torch drew near in the night; and the misshapen hands groped in the meshes of the net; and they took the missionary between the finger and the thumb, and bore him dripping in the night and silence to the place of the ovens of Miru. And there was Miru, ruddy in the glow of the ovens; and there sat her four daughters and made the kava of the dead; and there sat the comers out of the islands of the living dripping and lamenting.

This was a dread place to reach for any of the sons of men. But of all who ever came there, the missionary was the most concerned; and to make things worse the person next him was a convert of his own.

"Aha," said the convert, "so you are here like your neighbours? And how about all your stories?"

"It seems," said the missionary with bursting tears, "that there was nothing in them."

By this the kava of the dead was ready and

the daughters of Miru began to intone in the old manner of singing. " Gone are the green islands and the bright sea, the sun and the moon and the forty million stars, and life and love and hope. Henceforth is no more, only to sit in the night and silence, and see your friends devoured ; for life is a deceit and the bandage is taken from your eyes."

Now when the singing was done, one of the daughters came with the bowl. Desire of that kava rose in the missionary's bosom ; he lusted for it like a swimmer for the land, or a bridegroom for his bride ; and he reached out his hand, and took the bowl, and would have drunk. And then he remembered, and put it back.

" Drink ! " sang the daughter of Miru. " There is no kava like the kava of the dead, and to drink of it once is the reward of living."

" I thank you. It smells excellent," said the missionary. " But I am a blue-ribbon man myself; and though I am aware there is a difference of opinion even in our own confession, I have always held kava to be excluded."

" What ! " cried the convert. " Are you

going to respect a taboo **at a** time like this?
And you were always so opposed to taboos
when you were alive ! "

" To other people's," said the missionary.
" Never to my own."

" But yours have all proved wrong," **said**
the convert.

" It looks like it," said the missionary,
"and I can't help that. No reason why I
should break my word."

" I never heard the like of this ! " cried the
daughter of Miru. " Pray, what do you ex-
pect to gain ? "

" That is not the point," said the missionary. " I took this pledge for others, I am not
going to break **it** for myself."

The daughter of Miru was puzzled; **she**
came and told her mother, and Miru was
vexed ; and they went and told Akaänga.

" I don't know what to do about this," said
Akaänga; and he came and reasoned with **the**
missionary.

" But there *is* such **a thing** as right and
wrong," said the missionary ; "and your
ovens cannot **alter that.**"

"Give the kava to the rest," said Akaänga to the daughters of Miru. "I must get rid of this sea-lawyer instantly, or worse will come of it."

The next moment the missionary came up in the midst of the sea, and there before him were the palm trees of the island. He swam to the shore gladly, and landed. Much matter of thought was in that missionary's mind.

"I seem to have been misinformed upon some points," said he. "Perhaps there is not much in it as I supposed ; but there is something in it after all. Let me be glad of that."

And he rang the bell for service.

## MORAL.

The sticks break, the stones crumble,
The eternal altars tilt and tumble,
Sanctions and tales dislimn like mist
About the amazed evangelist.
He stands unshook from age to youth
Upon one pin-point of the truth.

# XVII.

## FAITH, HALF-FAITH, AND NO FAITH AT ALL.

IN the ancient days there went three men upon pilgrimage; one was a priest, and one was a virtuous person, and the third was an old rover with his axe.

As they went, the priest spoke about the grounds of faith.

"We find the proofs of our religion in the works of nature," said he, and beat his breast.

"That is true," said the virtuous person.

"The peacock has a scrannel voice," said the priest, "as has been laid down always in our books. How cheering!" he cried, in a voice like one that wept. "How comforting!"

"I require no such proofs," said the virtuous person.

"Then you have no reasonable faith," said the priest.

"Great is the right, and shall prevail!" cried the virtuous person. "There is loyalty in my soul; be sure, there is loyalty in the mind of Odin."

"These are but playings upon words," returned the priest. "A sackful of such trash is nothing to the peacock."

Just then they passed a country farm where there was a peacock seated on a rail, and the bird opened its mouth and sang with the voice of a nightingale.

"Where are you now?" asked the virtuous person. "And yet this shakes not me! Great is the truth and shall prevail!"

"The devil fly away with that peacock!" said the priest; and he was downcast for a mile or two.

But presently they came to a shrine, where a Fakeer performed miracles.

"Ah!" said the priest, "here are the true grounds of faith. The peacock was but an adminicle. This is the base of our religion." And he beat upon his breast and groaned like one with colic.

"Now to me," said the virtuous person,

"all this is as little to the purpose as the peacock. I believe because I see the right is great
and must prevail; and this Fakeer might carry
**on** with his conjuring tricks till doomsday, and
**it** would not play bluff upon a man like me."

Now at this the Fakeer was so much incensed
that his hand trembled ; and lo! in the midst
of a miracle the cards fell from up his sleeve.

"Where are you now?" asked the virtuous
person. "And yet it shakes not **me**!"

"The **devil fly away** with the Fakeer!"
cried the priest. "**I** really **do not see** the
good of going on with this pilgrimage."

"**Cheer up!**" cried the virtuous person.
"Great is the right and shall prevail!"

"If you are quite sure it will prevail?" **says**
the priest.

"I pledge my word **for that,**" said **the vir-**
tuous person.

So the other began to go on again **with a better** heart.

**At** last one **came** running, and **told** them all
was lost : that the powers of darkness had be-
sieged the Heavenly Mansions, that Odin was
to die, and evil triumph.

"I have been grossly deceived," cried the virtuous person.

"All is lost now," said the priest.

"I wonder if it is too late to make it up with the devil?" said the virtuous person.

"O, I hope not," said the priest. "And at any rate we can but try. But what are you doing with your axe?" says he to the rover.

"I am off to die with Odin," said the rover.

# XVIII.

## *THE TOUCHSTONE.*

THE King was a man that stood well before the world, his smile was sweet **as** clover, but his soul withinsides was as little **as** a pea. He had **two** sons; and **the** younger son was a boy after his heart, but the elder was one whom he feared. It befel one morning that the drum sounded in the dun before it was yet day; and the King rode with his two sons, **and a** brave array behind them. They rode two hours, and came to the foot **of a** brown mountain that was very steep.

"Where do **we** ride?" said the elder son.

Across this brown mountain," said the **King,** and smiled to himself.

"My father knows what **he is** doing," said the younger son.

And they rode two hours more, and came to the sides of a black river that was wondrous deep.

"And where do we ride?" asked the elder son.

"Over this black river," said the King, and smiled to himself.

"My father knows what he is doing," said the younger son.

And they rode all that day, and about the time of the sunsetting came to the side of a lake, where was a great dun.

"It is here we ride," said the King; "to a King's house, and a priest's, and a house where you will learn much."

At the gates of the dun, the King who was a priest met them, and he was a grave man, and beside him stood his daughter, and she was as fair as the morn, and one that smiled and looked down.

"These are my two sons," said the first King.

"And here is my daughter," said the King who was a priest.

"She is a wonderful fine maid," said the first King, "and I like her manner of smiling."

"They are wonderful well-grown lads," said the second, "and I like their gravity."

**And** then the two Kings looked **at** each
other, and said " The thing may come about."

And in the meanwhile the two lads looked
upon the maid, and the one grew pale and the
other red; **and** the maid looked **upon** the
ground smiling.

" Here is the maid that I shall marry," said
the elder. " For I think she smiled upon me."

But the younger plucked his father by the
sleeve. " Father," said he, " a word in **your**
ear. If I find favour in your sight, might not I
wed this maid, for I think she smiles upon me ? "

" A word in yours," said the King his
father. " Waiting is good hunting, and when
the teeth are shut the tongue is at home."

Now they were come into the dun, and
feasted; and this was a great house, so that
the lads were astonished; and the King **that**
was a priest sat at **the** end **of the** board and
was silent, so that the **lads** were filled with
reverence; **and the** maid served them smiling
with downcast eyes, so that their hearts were
enlarged.

Before it was day, the elder son arose, and
he found the maid at her weaving, for she was

a diligent girl. "Maid," quoth he, "I would fain marry you."

"You must speak with my father," said she, and she looked upon the ground smiling, and became like the rose.

"Her heart is with me," said the elder son, and he went down to the lake and sang.

A little after came the younger son. "Maid," quoth he, "if our fathers were agreed, I would like well to marry you."

"You can speak to my father," said she, and looked upon the ground and smiled and grew like the rose."

"She is a dutiful daughter," said the younger son, "she will make an obedient wife." And then he thought "What shall I do?" and he remembered the King her father was a priest; so he went into the temple and sacrificed a weasel and a hare.

Presently the news got about; and the two lads and the first King were called into the presence of the King who was a priest, where he sat upon the high seat.

"Little I reck of gear," said the King who was a priest, "and little of power. For we

live here among the shadows of things, and the
heart is sick of seeing them. And we stay
here in the wind like raiment drying, and the
heart is weary of the wind. But one thing I
love, and that **is** truth ; and for one thing will
I give my daughter, and that is the trial stone.
For in the light of that stone the seeming goes,
and the being shows, and all things besides
are worthless. Therefore, lads, **if** ye would
wed my daughter, out foot, and bring me **the**
stone of touch, **for that is** the price of her.''

" A word in your ear,'' said the younger son
to his **father.** "**I** think we do very well without this stone.''

"**A** word in yours,'' said his father. "**I
am of** your way of thinking ; but when **the**
teeth are shut the tongue is **at home.''** And
he smiled to the King that was a priest.

But the elder son got to his feet, and called
the King that was **a priest by** the name of
father. "For whether **I marry** the maid **or**
no, I will call you **by** that word for the love of
your wisdom ; and even now I will ride forth
and search the world for the stone of touch.''
So he said farewell and rode into the world.

5

"I think I will go, too," said the younger son, "if I can have your leave. For my heart goes out to the maid."

"You will ride home with me," said his father.

So they rode home, and when they came to the dun, the King had his son into his treasury. "Here," said he, "is the touchstone which shows truth; for there is no truth but plain truth; and if you will look in this, you will see yourself as you are."

And the younger son looked in it, and saw his face as it were the face of a beardless youth, and he was well enough pleased; for the thing was a piece of a mirror.

"Here is no such great thing to make a work about," said he; "but if it will get me the maid, I shall never complain. But what a fool is my brother to ride into the world, and the thing all the while at home."

So they rode back to the other dun, and showed the mirror to the King that was a priest; and when he had looked in it, and seen himself like a King, and his house like a King's house, and all things like themselves, he cried

out and blessed God. "For now I know,"
said he, "there is no truth but the plain truth;
and I am a King indeed, although my heart
misgave me." And he pulled down his temple,
and built a new one; and then the younger
son was married to the maid.

In the meantime the elder son rode into the
world to find the touchstone of the trial of
truth; and whenever he came to a place of
habitation, he would ask the men if they had
heard of it. And in every place the men answered: "Not only have we heard of it, but
we, alone of all men, possess the thing itself,
and it hangs in the side of our chimney to this
day." Then would the elder son be glad, and
beg for a sight of it. And sometimes it would
be a piece of mirror, that showed the seeming
of things, and then he would say, "This can
never be, for there should be more than seeming." And sometimes it would be a lump
of coal, which showed nothing; and then he
would say, "This can never be, for at least
there is the seeming." And sometimes it would
be a touchstone indeed, beautiful in hue,
adorned with polishing, the light inhabiting its

sides; and when **he** found **this,** he would beg **the** thing, and the persons of that place would give it him, for all men were **very** generous of that gift; **so that** at the last he **had** his wallet full **of them, and they** chinked together when he rode; **and when** he halted by the side of the way he would take **them out and try** them, till his head turned like **the sails** upon a windmill.

" A murrain upon this business ! " said the elder son, " for I perceive no end to it. Here I have the red, and here the blue and the green; and to me they seem all excellent, and yet shame each other. A murrain on the trade ! If it **were not** for the King that is a **priest and** whom I **have** called my father, and **if it were** not for the fair maid of the dun that **makes my mouth to** sing **and my heart** enlarge, I would **even** tumble them all into the salt **sea,** and go home and **be a** King like other folk."

But he **was like the** hunter that has seen a stag upon a mountain, **so** that the night may fall, and **the fire be** kindled **and** the lights **shine in his house,** but desire of that stag is single in his bosom.

**Now** after **many years** the elder son came

upon the sides of the salt sea ; and it was night, and a savage place, and the clamour of the sea was loud. There he was aware of a house, **and** a man that sat there by the light **of a** candle, for he had no **fire. Now** the elder son came in to him, and the man gave him water to drink, for he had no bread ; **and** wagged his head **when** he was spoken **to,** for he had no words.

" Have you the touchstone of **truth ? "** asked the elder son ; and when the man had wagged his **head, "** I might have known that," cried the elder son, " I have here a wallet full of them ! " And with that he laughed, although his heart was weary.

And with that the man laughed **too,** and with **the** fuff **of** his laughter the candle went out.

" Sleep," said **the man,** " **for now I** think you have **come far** enough ; **and** your quest **is** ended, and my candle is **out."**

**Now** when the morning came, the man gave him a clear pebble in his hand, and it had no beauty and no colour, and the elder son looked upon it scornfully and shook his head, and he

went away, for it seemed a small affair to
him.

All that day he rode, and his mind was quiet,
and the desire of the chase allayed. "How if
this poor pebble be the touchstone, after all?"
said he; and he got down from his horse, and
emptied forth his wallet by the side of the way.
Now, in the light of each other, all the touchstones lost their hue and fire and withered like
stars at morning; but in the light of the pebble their beauty remained, only the pebble was
the most bright. And the elder son smote
upon his brow. "How if this be the truth?"
he cried, "that all are a little true?" And
he took the pebble, and turned its light upon
the heavens, and they deepened above him like
the pit; and he turned it on the hills, and the
hills were cold and rugged, but life ran in their
sides so that his own life bounded; and he
turned it on the dust, and he beheld the dust
with joy and terror; and he turned it on himself, and kneeled down and prayed.

"Now thanks be to God," said the elder
son, "I have found the touchstone; and now
I may turn my reins, and ride home to the

King and to the maid of the dun that makes
my mouth to sing and my heart enlarge.''

Now when he came to the dun, he saw children playing by the gate where the King had
met him in the old days ; and this stayed his
pleasure, for he thought in his heart, '' It is
here my children should be playing.'' **And**
when he came into the hall, there was **his**
brother on the high seat and the maid beside
him ; and at that his anger rose, for he thought
in his heart, '' **It is I** that should **be** sitting
there, and the maid beside me.''

'' Who are you ? '' said his brother.  '' And
what make you in the dun ? ''

'' **I am** your elder brother,'' he replied.
'' And **I am** come to marry the maid, for I
have brought the touchstone of truth.''

Then the younger brother laughed aloud.
'' Why,'' said he, '' I found the touchstone
years ago, and married the maid, and there are
our children playing at the gate.''

Now **at** this the elder brother grew as gray
as the dawn.  '' I pray you have dealt justly,''
said he, '' for I perceive my life is lost.''

'' Justly ? '' quoth the younger brother.  '' **It**

becomes you ill, that are a restless man and a
runagate, to doubt my justice or the King my
father's that are sedentary folk and known in
the land.''

" Nay,'' said the elder brother, " you have
all else, have patience also ; and suffer me to
say the world is full of touchstones, and it ap-
pears not easily which is true.''

"I have no shame of mine,'' said the
younger brother.   "There it is, and look in
it.''

So the elder brother looked in the mirror,
and he was sore amazed ; for he was an old
man, and his hair was white upon his head ;
and he sat down in the hall and wept aloud.

" Now,'' said the younger brother, " see
what a fool's part you have played, that ran
over all the world to seek what was lying in
our father's treasury, and came back an old
carle for the dogs to bark at, and without chick
or child.   And I that was dutiful and wise sit
here crowned with virtues and pleasures, and
happy in the light of my hearth.''

" Methinks you have a cruel tongue,'' said
the elder brother ; and he pulled out the clear

pebble and turned its light on his brother ; and behold the man was lying, his soul was shrunk into the smallness of a pea, and his heart was **a bag of** little fears like scorpions, and **love** was dead in his bosom. And **at** that the elder brother cried out aloud, and turned **the** light of the pebble on the maid, and lo ! she was but **a** mask of a woman, and withinsides she was quite dead, and she smiled as a clock ticks **and** knew not wherefore.

" Oh, well," said **the** elder brother, " I perceive there is both good and bad. So fare ye all **as** well as ye may in the dun ; but I will go forth into the world with **my** pebble in my **pocket.**"

# XIX.

## THE POOR THING.

THERE was a man in the islands who fished for his bare bellyful, and took his life in his hands to go forth upon the sea between four planks. But though he had much ado, he was merry of heart; and the gulls heard him laugh when the spray met him. And though he had little lore, he was sound of spirit; and when the fish came to his hook in the midwaters, he blessed God without weighing. He was bitter poor in goods and bitter ugly of countenance, and he had no wife.

It fell in the time of the fishing, that the man awoke in his house about the midst of the afternoon. The fire burned in the midst, and the smoke went up and the sun came down by the chimney. And the man was aware of the likeness of one that warmed his hands at the red peats.

"I greet you," said the man, "in the name of God."

"I greet **you**," **said he** that warmed his hands, "**but** not in the name of God, for I am none of His; nor in the name of Hell, for I am not **of** Hell. For I am but **a** bloodless thing, less than wind and lighter than a sound, and the wind goes through me like a net, and I am broken by **a** sound and shaken **by** the cold."

"Be plain **with me**," said the **man**, "and tell me your name and of your nature."

"**My** name," quoth the other, "is **not** yet named, and my nature not yet sure. For I am **part of a man;** and I was a part of **your** fathers, **and went** out to fish **and** fight with them in the ancient days. But now is my **turn** not yet come; and I **wait** until **you** have **a** wife, and then shall I be **in your** son, and a brave part of him, rejoicing manfully to launch the boat into the surf, skilful to direct the helm, and **a** man of might where the **ring** closes **and** the blows **are** going."

"This is a marvellous thing to hear," said the man; "and if **you** are indeed to be my son, **I fear** it **will go** ill **with you;** for I am bitter poor in goods and bitter ugly in face, and I shall never get me a wife if I live to the age of eagles."

"All this have I come to remedy, my Father," said the Poor Thing; "for we must go this night to the little isle of sheep, where our fathers lie in the dead-cairn, and to-morrow to the Earl's Hall, and there shall you find a wife by my providing."

So the man rose and put forth his boat at the time of the sunsetting; and the Poor Thing sat in the prow, and the spray blew through his bones like snow, and the wind whistled in his teeth, and the boat dipped not with the weight of him.

"I am fearful to see you, my son," said the man. "For methinks you are no thing of God."

"It is only the wind that whistles in my teeth," said the Poor Thing, "and there is no life in me to keep it out."

So they came to the little isle of sheep, where the surf burst all about it in the midst of the sea, and it was all green with bracken, and all wet with dew, and the moon enlightened it.

They ran the boat into a cove, and set foot to land; and the man came heavily behind among the rocks in the deepness of the bracken, but the Poor Thing went before him like a smoke in the light of the moon. So they came to the dead-cairn, and they laid their ears to the stones; and the dead complained withinsides like a swarm of bees: " Time was that marrow was in our bones, and strength in our sinews; and the thoughts of our head were clothed upon with acts and the words of men. But now are we broken in sunder, and the bonds of our bones are loosed, and our thoughts lie in the dust."

" Then said the Poor Thing : " Charge them that they give you the virtue they withheld."

And the man said : " Bones of my fathers, greeting ! for I am sprung of your loins. And now behold I break open the piled stones of your cairn, and I let in the noon between your ribs. Count it well done, for it was to be; and give me what I come seeking in the name of blood and in the name of God."

And the spirits of the dead stirred in the cairn like ants; and they spoke : " You have

broken the roof of our cairn and let in the noon
between our ribs; and you have the strength
of the still-living.   But what virtue have we?
what power? or what jewel here in the dust
with us, that any living man should covet or
receive it? for we are less than nothing.   But
we tell you one thing, speaking with many
voices like bees, that the way is plain before
all like the grooves of launching: So forth into
life and fear not, for so did we all in the ancient ages."   And their voices passed away like
an eddy in a river.

"Now," said the Poor Thing, "they have
told you a lesson, but make them give you a
gift.   Stoop your hand among the bones without drawback, and you shall find their treasure."

So the man stooped his hand, and the dead
laid hold upon it many and faint like ants; but
he shook them off, and behold, what he brought
up in his hand was the shoe of a horse, and it
was rusty.

" It is a thing of no price," quoth the man,
" for it is rusty."

" We shall see that," said the Poor Thing;

" for in my thought **it is a** good thing **to** do what our fathers did, and **to** keep what **they** kept without question. And in my thought one thing is as good as another **in** this **world ;** and a shoe of a horse will do."

Now they got into their boat with the horse-shoe, and when the dawn was come they were aware of the smoke of the Earl's town and the bells of the Kirk that beat. So they set **foot to** shore ; and the man **went up** to the market among the fishers over against the palace and the Kirk ; and he was bitter poor and bitter ugly, and **he** had never a fish to sell, but only a shoe of a horse in his creel, and it rusty.

" Now," said the Poor **Thing,** " do so and **so,** and you shall find **a** wife **and** I a mother."

It befell that the Earl's daughter came forth **to** go into the Kirk upon her prayers, and when she saw the poor man stand in the market with only the shoe of a horse, and it rusty, it came in her mind it should **be** a thing of price.

" What is that ? " quoth she.

" It is a shoe of a horse," said the man.

" And what is **the** use of it ? " quoth the Earl's daughter.

"It is for no use," said the man.

"I may not believe that," said she; "else why should you carry it?"

"I do so," said he, "because it was so my fathers did in the ancient ages; and I have neither a better reason nor a worse."

Now the Earl's daughter could not find it in her mind to believe him. "Come," quoth she, "sell me this, for I am sure it is a thing of price."

"Nay," said the man, "the thing is not for sale."

"What!" cried the Earl's daughter. "Then what make you here in the town's market, with the thing in your creel and nought beside?"

"I sit here," says the man, "to get me a wife."

"There is no sense in any of these answers," thought the Earl's daughter; "and I could find it in my heart to weep."

By came the Earl upon that; and she called him and told him all. And when he had heard, he was of his daughter's mind that this should be a thing of virtue; and charged the man to

set a price upon the thing or else be hanged
upon the gallows, and that was near at hand so
that the man could see it.

" The way of life is straight like the grooves
of launching," quoth the man. " And if I am
to be hanged let me be hanged."

" Why ! " cried the Earl, " **will** you **set**
your neck against a shoe of **a** horse, and it
rusty ? "

" In **my thought,**" said the man, "**one**
thing **is** as good as another in this world ; and
a shoe of a horse will do."

" This can never be," thought the Earl, and
he stood and looked upon the man, and bit his
beard.

And the man looked up at him and smiled.
" It was so my fathers did in the ancient ages,"
quoth he to the Earl, " **and** I have neither **a**
better reason **nor a worse.**"

" There is no **sense in** any of this," thought
the Earl, " **and I** must be growing old." So
he had his daughter on one side, and says he :
" Many suitors have you denied, my child.
But here is a very strange matter that **a** man
should cling **so to a** shoe **of a** horse, and it

rusty ; and that he should offer it like a thing
on sale, and yet not sell it ; and that he should
sit there seeking a wife.   If I come not to the
bottom of this thing, I shall have no more
pleasure in bread ; and I can see no way, but
either I should hang or you should marry
him.''

"By my troth, but he is bitter ugly," said
the Earl's daughter.   "How if the gallows be
so near at hand ?"

"It was not so," said the Earl, "that my
fathers did in the ancient ages.   I am like the
man, and can give you neither a better reason
nor a worse.   But do you, prithee, speak with
him again."

So the Earl's daughter spoke to the man.
"If you were not so bitter ugly," quoth she,
"my father the Earl would have us marry."

"Bitter ugly am I," said the man, "and
you as fair as May.   Bitter ugly I am, and
what of that ?   It was so my fathers   .   .   ."

"In the name of God," said the Earl's
daughter, "let your fathers be !"

"If I had done that," said the man, "you
had never been chaffering with me here in the

market, nor your father the Earl watching with the end of his eye.''

'' But come,'' quoth the Earl's daughter, ''this a very strange thing, that you would **have** me wed for a shoe **of** a horse, and it rusty.''

'' In my thought,'' quoth the man, '' one thing is **as good** . . .''

'' O, spare me that,'' said the Earl's daughter, ''and tell me why I should marry.''

'' Listen and look,'' **said** the man.

Now the wind blew through the Poor Thing like an infant crying, so that her heart was melted ; and her eyes were unsealed, and **she** was aware of the thing as it **were** a babe un-**mothered,** and she took it to her arms, and it melted in her arms like the air.

'' Come,'' said the man, '' **behold a** vision of our children, the busy hearth, and the white heads. And **let that** suffice, for it is all God offers.''

'' I have no delight **in** it,'' said she, but with that she sighed.

'' The ways of life **are** straight like the grooves of launching,'' **said the** man, **and he** took her by the hand.

"And what shall we do with the horse-shoe?" quoth she.

"I will give it to your father," said the man; "and he can make a Kirk and a mill of it for me."

It came to pass in time that the Poor Thing was born, but memory of these matters slept within him, and he knew not that which he had done. But he was a part of the eldest son; rejoicing manfully to launch the boat into the surf, skilful to direct the helm, and a man of might where the ring closes and the blows are going.

## XX

## *THE SONG OF THE MORROW.*

THE King of Duntrine had a daughter
when he was old, and **she** was the fair-
est King's daughter between two seas; **her**
hair was like spun gold and her eyes like pools
in a river; and the King gave her a castle upon the sea beach, with a terrace, and a court
of the hewn stone, and four towers at the four
corners. Here she dwelt and grew up, and
had no care for the morrow and no power
upon the hour, after the manner of simple men.

It befell that she walked one day by the
beach of the sea, when it was autumn, and the
wind blew from the place of rains; and upon
the one hand **of** her the sea beat, and upon the
other the dead leaves ran. This was the lone-
liest beach between two seas, and strange things
had been done there in the ancient ages. Now
**the** King's daughter was aware of a crone that

sat upon the beach. The sea foam ran to her
feet, and the dead leaves swarmed about her
back, and the rags blew about her face in the
blowing of the wind.

"Now," said the King's daughter, and she
named a holy name, "this is the most unhappy
old crone between two seas."

"Daughter of a King," said the crone,
"you dwell in a stone house, and your hair is
like the gold, but what is your profit? Life is
not long, nor lives strong; and you live after
the way of simple men, and have no thought
for the morrow and no power upon the hour."

"Thought for the morrow, that I have," said
the King's daughter; "but power upon the hour,
that have I not." And she mused with herself.

Then the crone smote her lean hands one
within the other, and laughed like a seagull.
"Home," cried she, "O daughter of a King,
home to your stone house, for the longing is
come upon you now, nor can you live any
more after the manner of simple men. Home,
and toil and suffer, till the gift come that will
make you bare, and till the man come that will
bring you care."

The King's daughter made no **more ado,** but she turned about and went home to her house in silence. And when she was come into her chamber she called for her nurse.

" Nurse," said the King's daughter, " thought is come upon me for the morrow, so that I can live no more after the manner of simple men. Tell me what I must do that **I may** have power upon the hour."

Then the nurse moaned like a snow wind. " Alas ! " said she, " that this thing should be ; but the thought is gone into your marrow, nor is there any cure against the thought. Be **it** so, then, even as you will ; though power is less than weakness, power shall you have ; and though the thought is colder than winter, yet shall you think it to an end."

**So the** King's daughter **sat in her** vaulted chamber in the masoned house, and she thought upon the thought. Nine years she sat ; and **the sea** beat upon **the** terrace, and the gulls cried about the turrets, and wind crooned in **the** chimneys of the house. Nine years she came not abroad, nor tasted the clean air, neither saw God's sky. Nine years she sat and looked neither to the right nor to the left, nor heard speech of anyone, but thought upon the thought of the morrow. And her nurse fed her in silence, and she took of the food with her left hand and ate it without grace.

Now when the nine years were out, it fell dusk in the autumn, and there came a sound in the wind like a sound of piping. At that the nurse lifted up her finger in the vaulted house.

"I hear a sound in the wind," said she, "that is like the sound of piping."

"It is but a little sound," said the King's daughter, "but yet is it sound enough for me."

So they went down in the dusk to the doors of the house, and along the beach of the sea. And the waves beat upon the one hand, and upon the other the dead leaves ran; and the clouds raced in the sky, and the gulls flew widdershins. And when they came to that part of the beach where strange things had been done in the ancient ages, lo, there was the crone, and she was dancing widdershins.

"What makes you dance widdershins, old crone?" said the King's daughter, "here upon the bleak beach between the waves and the dead leaves? ''

" I hear a sound in the wind that is like a sound of piping," quoth she. " And it is for that that I dance widdershins. For the gift comes that will make you bare, and the man comes that must bring you care. But for me the morrow is come that I have thought upon, and the hour of my power."

" How comes it, crone," said the King's daughter, " that you waver like a rag, and pale like a dead leaf before my eyes? ''

" Because the morrow has come that I have thought upon, and the hour of my power," said the crone, and she fell on the beach, and lo! she was but stalks of the sea tangle, and dust of the sea sand, and the sand lice hopped upon the place of her.

" This is the strangest thing that befell between two seas," said the King's daughter of Duntrine.

But the nurse broke out and moaned like an autumn gale. " I am weary of the wind," quoth she, and she bewailed her day.

The King's daughter was aware of a man

upon the beach, he went hooded so that none might perceive his face ; and a pipe was underneath his arm. The sound of his pipe was like singing wasps and like the wind that sings in windlestraw ; and it took hold upon men's ears like the crying of gulls.

"Are you the comer?" quoth the King's daughter of Duntrine.

"I am the come," said he, "and these are the pipes that a man may hear, and I have power upon the hour, and this is the song of the morrow." And he piped the song of the morrow, and it was as long as years, and the nurse wept out aloud at the hearing of it.

"This is true," said the King's daughter, "that you pipe the song of the morrow; but that ye have power upon the hour, how may I know that? Show me a marvel here upon the beach between the waves and the dead leaves."

And the man said "Upon whom?"

"Here is my nurse," quoth the King's daughter. "She is weary of the wind. Show me a good marvel upon her."

And lo the nurse fell upon the beach as it were two handfuls of dead leaves, and the wind whirled them widdershins, and the sand lice hopped between.

"It is true," said the King's daughter of Duntrine; "you are the comer, and you have power upon the hour. Come with me to my stone house."

So they went by the sea margin, **and the** man piped the song of **the** morrow, and **the** leaves followed behind them as **they went.** Then they sat **down** together; and the **sea** beat on the terrace, and the gulls cried about the towers, and the wind crooned in the chimneys **of** the house. Nine years they sat, and every year when it fell autumn, the man said, "This is **the** hour, and I have power in it," and the daughter of the King said, "Nay, but pipe me the song of the morrow." And **he** piped it, and it was long like years.

Now when the nine years were gone, the King's daughter of Duntrine got her to her feet, like one that remembers; and she looked about her in the masoned house; and all her servants **were** gone; only the man that piped sat upon the terrace with the hand upon his face, and as he piped the leaves ran about the terrace and the sea beat along the wall.  Then she cried to him with a great voice, " This is the hour, and let me see the power of it." And with that the wind blew off the hand from the man's face, and lo, there was no man there, only the clothes and the hand and the pipes tumbled one upon another in a corner of the terrace, and the dead leaves ran over them.

And the King's daughter of Duntrine got her to that part of the beach where strange things had been done in the ancient ages, and there she sat her down.  The sea foam ran to her feet, and the dead leaves swarmed about her back, and the veil blew about her face in the blowing of the wind.  And when she lifted up her eyes, there was the daughter of a King come walking on the beach.  Her hair was like the spun gold, and her eyes like pools in a river, and she had no thought for the morrow and no power upon the hour, after the manner of simple men.

www.ingramcontent.com/pod-product-compliance
Lightning Source LLC
Chambersburg PA
CBHW032158010726
47493CB00008BA/2738